SWEETUS · SHMEGEGGIUM

The Wand and the Sword

Mike Zarb
Robin Gold

RANDOM HOUSE AUSTRALIA

A Random House book
Published by Random House Australia Pty Ltd
Level 3, 100 Pacific Highway, North Sydney NSW 2060
www.randomhouse.com.au

First published by Random House Australia in 2009
Copyright © Robin Gold 2009
Illustration copyright © Mike Zarb 2009

National Library of Australia
Cataloguing-in-Publication Entry
    Author: Gold, Robin
    Title: The wand and the sword/Gold, Robin; illustrated by Mike Zarb.
    ISBN: 978 1 74166 321 1 (pbk.)
    Series: Gold, Robin. Belmont and the dragon; 2
    Target Audience: For primary school age.
    Other Authors/Contributors: Zarb, Mike.
    Dewey number: A823.4

Cover illustrations by Mike Zarb
Cover and text design and layout by Jobi Murphy
Printed and bound by 1010 Printing International Limited
10 9 8 7 6 5 4 3 2 1

For Joanne and Peter – MZ

To my mother and father – RG

Long ago in the madcap medieval metropolis of Old York, there lived a small boy named Belmont and a very large dragon named Burnie.

Every second Tuesday was half-price day for dragons at
the art museum, so one morning the two friends decided
to go along.

'This is my favourite picture in the whole place,' said Belmont. 'It's King Arthur, the legendary king of Camelot. And that's Excalibur!'

'Ex-what-a-who?' asked Burnie.

'Excalibur,' said Belmont. 'King Arthur's magical sword.'

Nearby, Mr Snerdley, the museum's curator, led a group of visitors to a priceless exhibit. 'And here is the centrepiece of our collection,' said Mr Snerdley, 'the magical wand of Merlin the Wizard. It is said that whoever possesses this wand has the power to control mighty kingdoms.'

'Let me get this straight, Sonny,' said a little old lady at the front. 'Could somebody use this wand to … let's say … take control of Old York, for instance?'

'Well, yes. I suppose so …' said Mr Snerdley.

'That's all I need to know, Ducky.'

There was a flash of light and a puff of red smoke.

'Sweet *shmegeggy*!' exclaimed Burnie. 'It's the Redwitch!'

The Redwitch snatched the wand from its display case. 'Old York is mine ... ALL MINE!' She kissed the wand with a loud SMACK.

'Yecch!' grumbled the wand. 'Take a breath mint, will ya?'

Alarms rang out from the museum as the Redwitch sped towards the palace on her broomstick. The king's brave knights gave chase but, with a wave of the stolen wand, the witch transformed them into brightly coloured bouncing beach balls.

'Works like a charm,' she sniggered.

King Cyrus and Princess Libby were playing a quiet
game of chess when the Redwitch burst through the
palace window.

'Okay, Pops,' said the Redwitch. 'As of now,
I'm taking over the joint, so you and
Doll Face can go take a hike.'

'Guards!' called the king.

Armed guards rushed into the room.

'Chopped liver on pumpernickel!' the witch commanded, and the guards became tasty snacks on a plate.

'What, no pickle?' she said.

King Cyrus drew his sword but, in a
flash, the deadly weapon was turned
into a swarm of butterflies.

The Redwitch whistled and a gaggle of ghastly goblins marched in, armed to the teeth. 'Throw 'em in the dungeon,' she commanded, 'and put in some extra rats!'

'You won't get away with this!' cried the king.

'I already have, Toots,' said the witch as the king and the princess were led away.

'Mmmm … something's missing,' said the Redwitch,
easing herself onto the throne. 'Aha! I've got it!'

With a touch of the wand, her
pointed hat became a golden crown.

'That's more like it,' she said.

'The situation is very serious,'
Mr Snerdley explained to a reporter.
'Merlin's wand has astonishing powers.
Only the legendary Excalibur was
more powerful.'

'Say, ain't that the name of King Artichoke's magical sword?' asked Burnie.

'You mean King *Arthur*? Yes, indeed,' said Mr Snerdley. 'It was said that whoever held Excalibur could vanquish any foe!'

'Even the Redwitch and that screwy wand?' asked the reporter.

'Yes. Without a doubt, Excalibur would prevail,' said Mr Snerdley.

'Then we've got to get hold of it somehow,' said Belmont.

Mr Snerdley took an old parchment map from an ancient cabinet. 'Excalibur is long lost, I'm afraid. It was cast into this lake, centuries ago.'

'May I borrow the map please, Mr Snerdley?' asked
Belmont. 'I promise I'll find Excalibur and, when
I do, I'm coming back for the Redwitch!'

'Well, I'll be a monkey's uncle,' said the reporter,
'the little nipper's got pluck!'

'Take it,' said Mr Snerdley, 'and good luck. You'll need it.'

'Mind if I tag along?' asked the reporter. 'I've got a nose
for news, and something tells me this is BIG, or
my name isn't Scoop O'Malley, ace reporter
for the *Old York Times*.'

'Be our guest, Mr O'Malley,' said
Belmont. 'We'll be leaving
without delay.'

OLD
YORK

N

W   E

S

ABOMINABLE
SNOWMAN

FOREST
OF
DOOM AND GLOOM

VON TRAPS

QUICKSANDS

CAMELOT

DUST
STORM

BLIZZARD

GREAT WALL
OF
CHINA DOLLS

WHIRLPOOL

DEATH ADDER
VALLEY

HAUNTED
SWAMP

PIRANHA
LAKE

'According to this map,' said Belmont, 'we're in Camelot and the lake ought to be right here.'

'But there's nothing but sand and rubble for miles,' said Scoop.

'Let's face it, kid,' said Burnie, 'we'll never find that sword … not in a million years.' With that, he tripped over something stuck in the dry lake bed.

'EXCALIBUR!' cried Belmont.

'Well, I'll be a monkey's uncle,' said Scoop.

'I *knew* we'd find it, kid!' said Burnie.

Belmont grasped the hilt of the sword.

'Hold it right there, small fry,' growled a voice from behind.

The companions turned to see two of the ugliest trolls they had ever laid eyes on. One held a crossbow aimed directly at them.

'You tie 'em up while I keep 'em covered,' said the first troll. 'After twenty years of searching, I don't aim for some pint-sized kid to snatch this prize away from me.'

With the prisoners safely bound, he grasped the hilt
of Excalibur and heaved with all his might, sweat
pouring from his brow. But the sword would not budge.
Exhausted, the troll sat down heavily on a strange
looking rock …

But it *wasn't* a rock. With a fearsome roar, a gigantic monster emerged from the sand.

It reared up to its full height and charged at the trolls.
They ran for their lives, screaming in terror with the
monster snapping at their heels.

The sun blazed down on the deserted captives and vultures circled overhead.

'Guess this is it, kid,' said Burnie. 'No shade. No food. No water. And not a decent soy latte for miles. It's only a matter of time now ...'

'It's all my fault!' blubbered Scoop. 'If I hadn't bribed a guard to let the Redwitch escape, none of this would have happened.'

'You did WHAAAT?' cried Burnie.

'Why would you do such a thing, Mr O'Malley?!' said Belmont.

'My career was on the skids. I needed a really big story to put me back on top. I never meant for *this* to happen,' Scoop sobbed.

'Never mind about that now,' said Belmont, as he struggled to his feet. 'I have an idea.'

With great difficulty he hopped over to Excalibur and began rubbing his ropes against the razor-sharp blade. The ropes fell away and he rushed over to untie Burnie and Scoop.

HOP   HOP   HOP

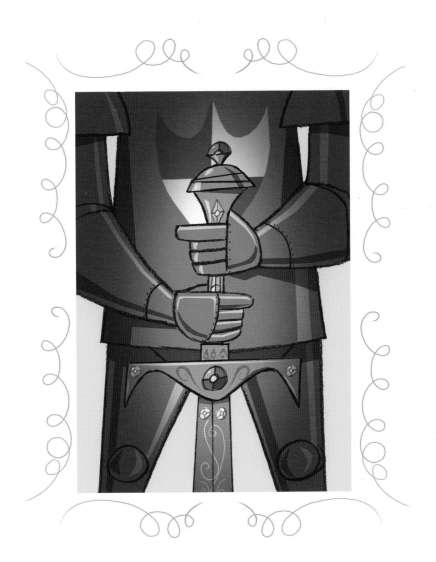

'Now for the sword,' said Belmont. He grasped the hilt of the mighty Excalibur …

and it slid out of the rock with ease!

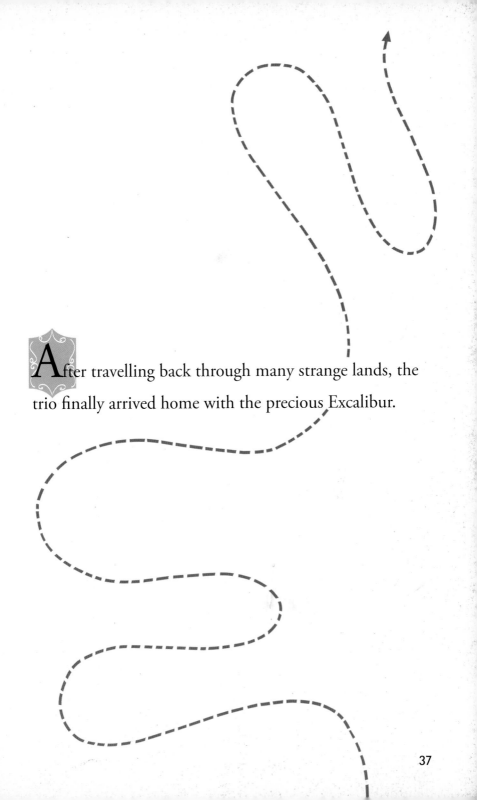

After travelling back through many strange lands, the trio finally arrived home with the precious Excalibur.

But something was amiss. Instead of the vibrant madcap metropolis they had left behind, Old York was now in ruins.

Belmont approached a man dressed in rags and saw that it was the museum curator.

'Mr Snerdley, what happened to Old York?!'

'The Redwitch … that's what happened,' he replied sadly as he walked away.

Suddenly, a haunting musical note filled the air.

'I think Excalibur is trying to tell us something,' said Belmont. 'But what?'

'Hey, you knuckleheads,' snapped Excalibur. 'Can't you see we're surrounded by goblin guards?'

In the palace, King Cyrus and Princess Libby stood bravely before the Redwitch.

'One little wave of this wand,' she cackled, 'and you'll soon be a couple of fat, juicy mice for Salem's supper.'

Just then the goblin guards marched in with Belmont, Burnie and Scoop.

'Well, well, well,' said the Redwitch, 'looks like Salem's getting a few extra courses tonight …'

The Redwitch raised her wand and a bolt of lightning flashed towards the prisoners.

'GERONIMO!' cried Belmont, as he threw himself in front of the princess. The bolt struck Excalibur's blade and bounced back at the witch, hitting her square in the kisser!

In a blinding flash, the Redwitch was changed into a fat, juicy mouse wearing a tiny crown. The cat's eyes widened as it slowly licked its chops.

'Salem! It's me, Mumsy-wumsy!' squeaked the mouse. 'Nice kitty. *Good kitty* …!' The little mouse scurried away, with the drooling cat in hot pursuit.

Belmont presented Excalibur to the king.

'Sire, I think you should lock this away somewhere safe.'

'Thank you, my boy,' said King Cyrus. 'You've done the kingdom a great service.'

Scoop O'Malley picked up the wand and studied it thoughtfully. 'I can see the headlines now: "Ace Reporter Finds Excalibur and Defeats the Redwitch! Hailed as Hero! – World Exclusive by Scoop O'Malley"!'

'Careful with that wand, Mr O'Malley,' said Belmont.

'Relax, Sonny. I know what I'm doing,' said Scoop.

'Put me down before somebody gets hurt, you big dope,' snapped the wand.

'Well, I'll be a monkey's uncle,' said Scoop.

Instantly, Scoop was transformed into a large, hairy monkey's uncle.

King Cyrus, Princess Libby and Belmont gasped with astonishment.

'All things considered,' said Burnie,
'I'd say that's an improvement.'